When I Was One

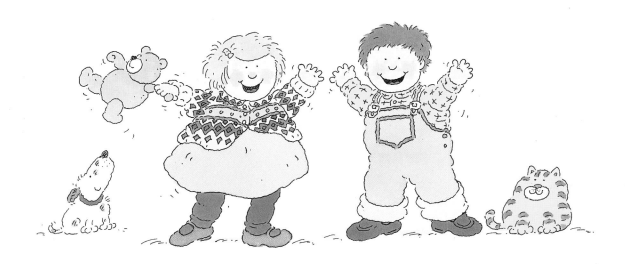

Colin and Jacqui Hawkins

VIKING

1

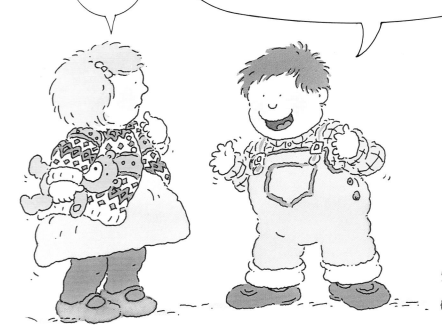
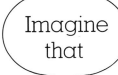

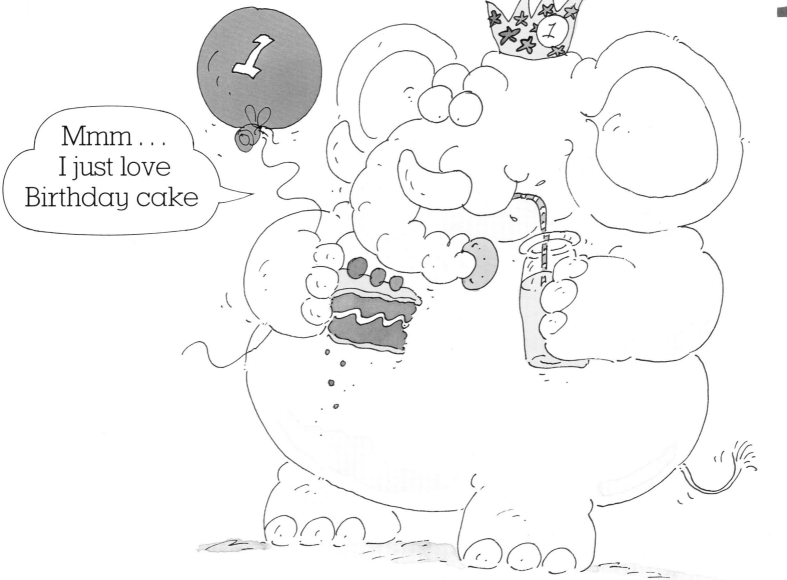

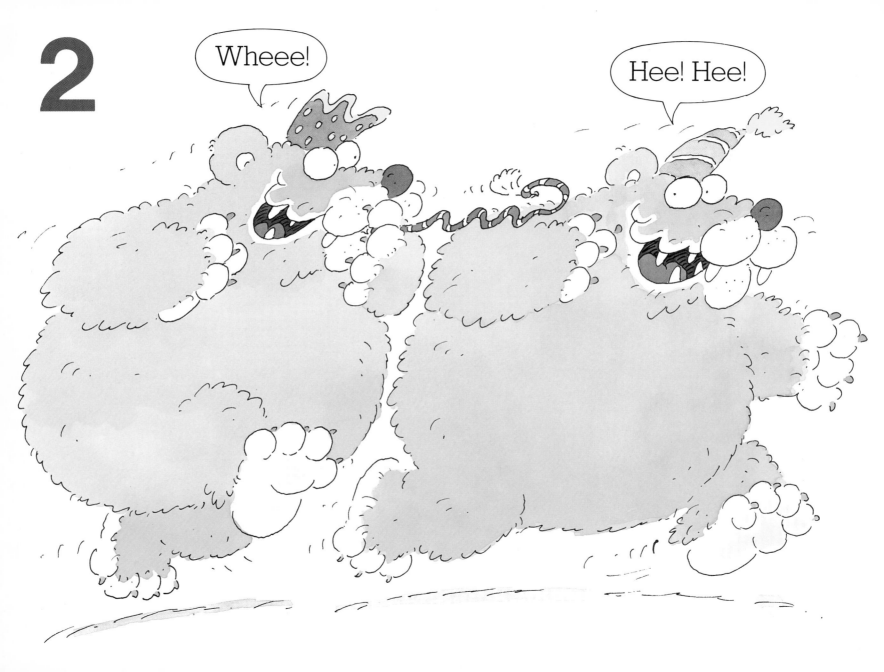

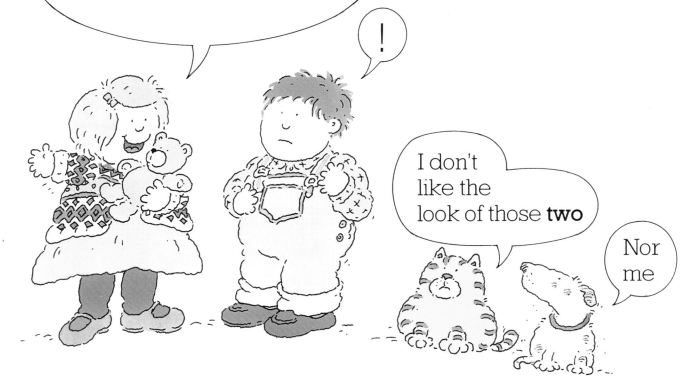

2

3

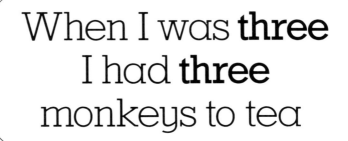

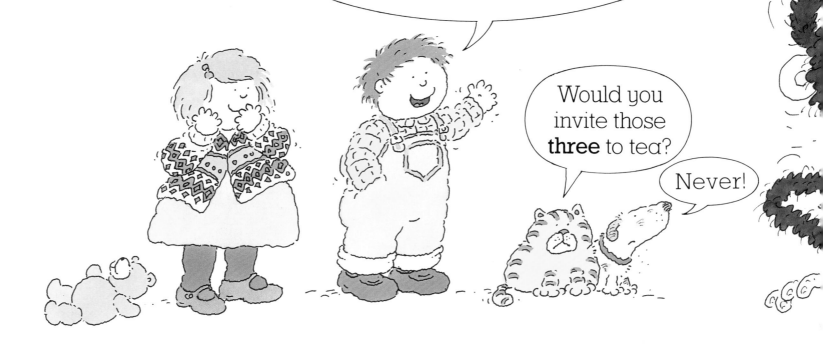

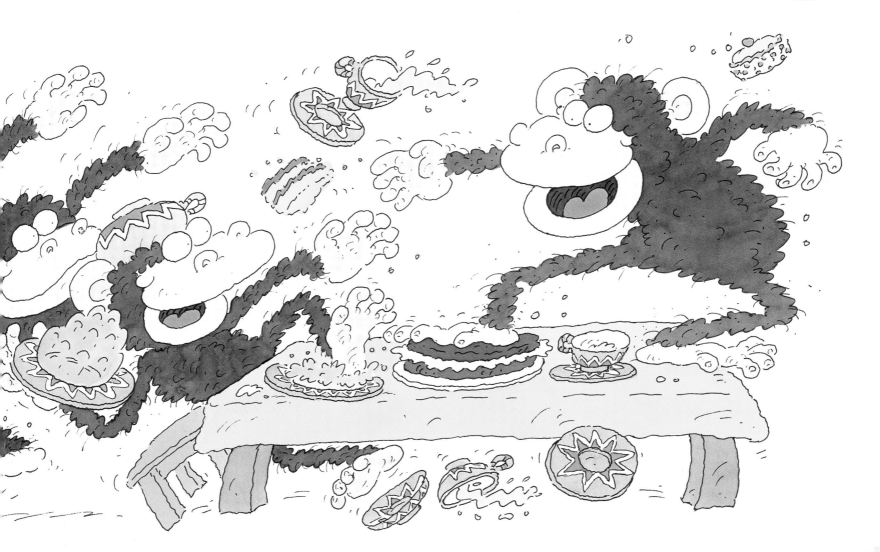

3

4

Slurp!

Munch!

Slurp!

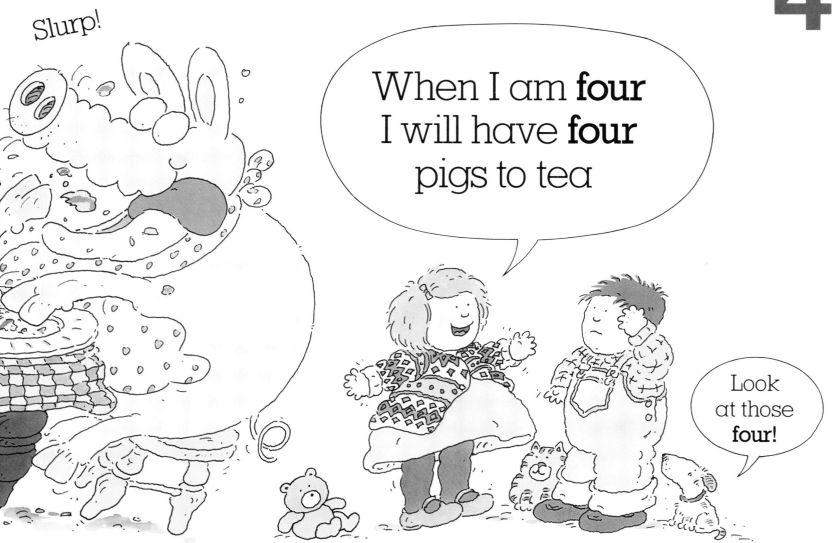

5

Well, when I am **five** I will go to school with **five** donkeys

?

Wait for me, Neddy

!

I bet they can't count up to **five**

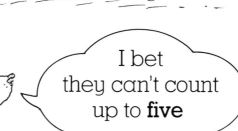

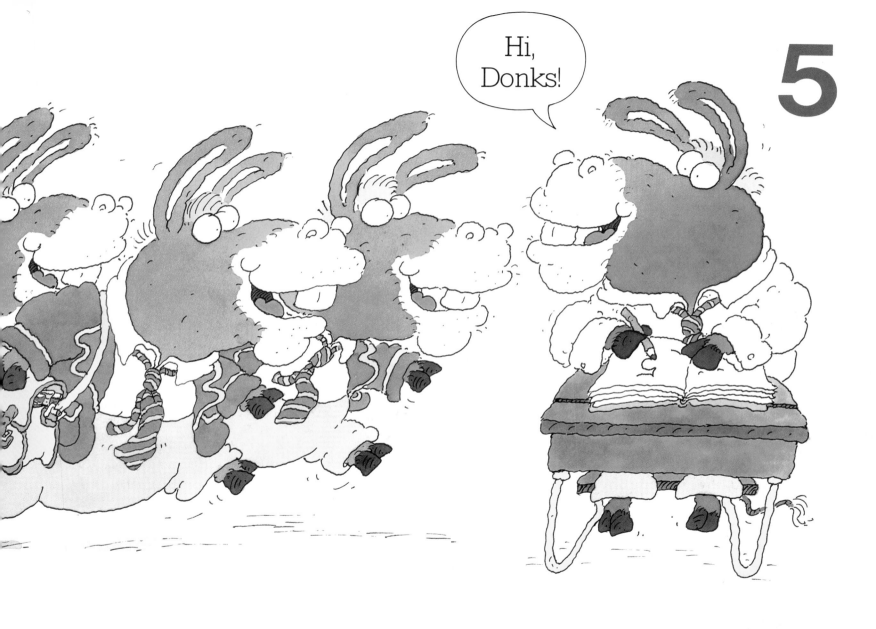

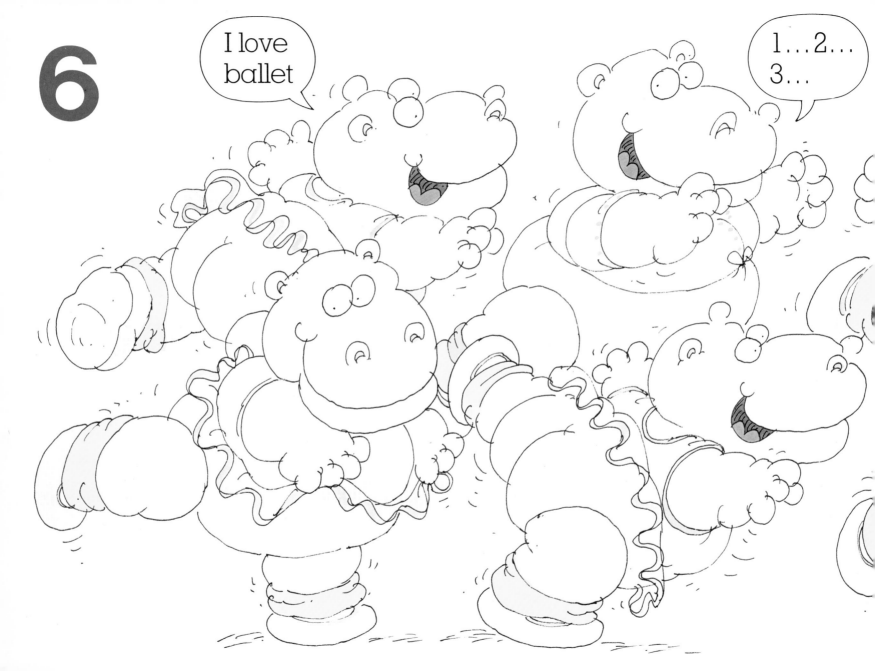

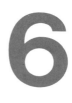

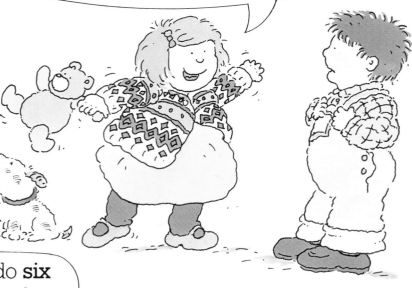

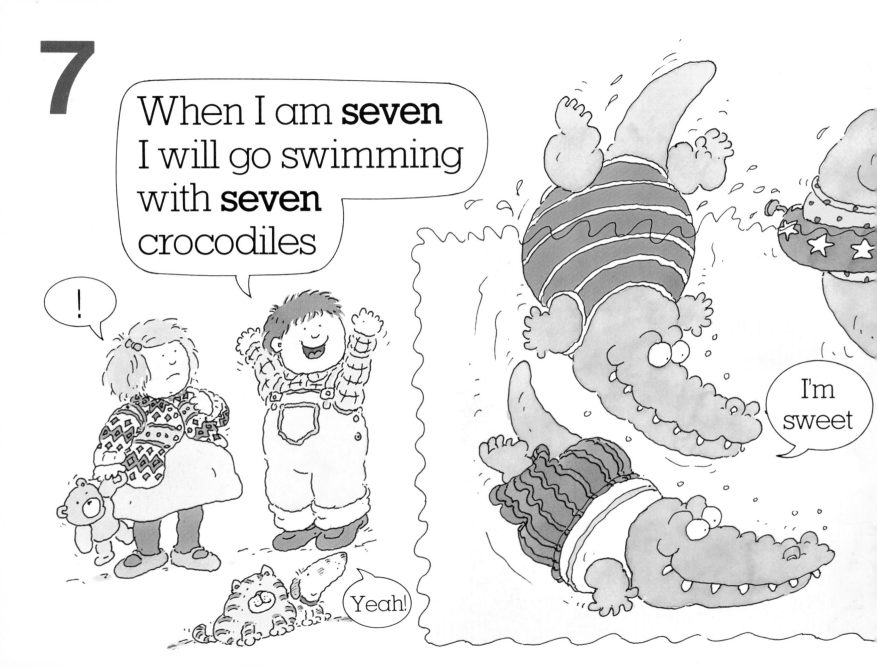

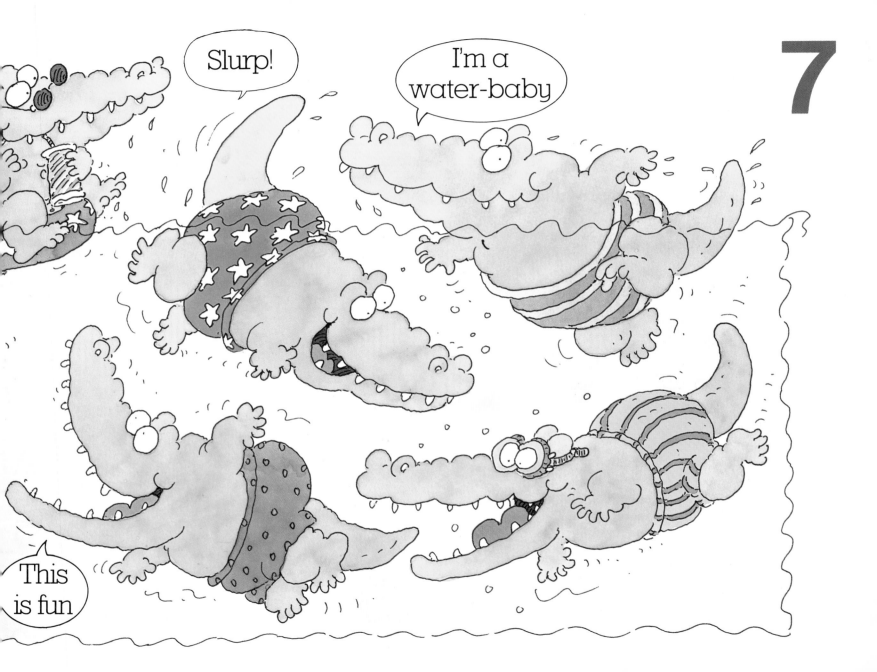

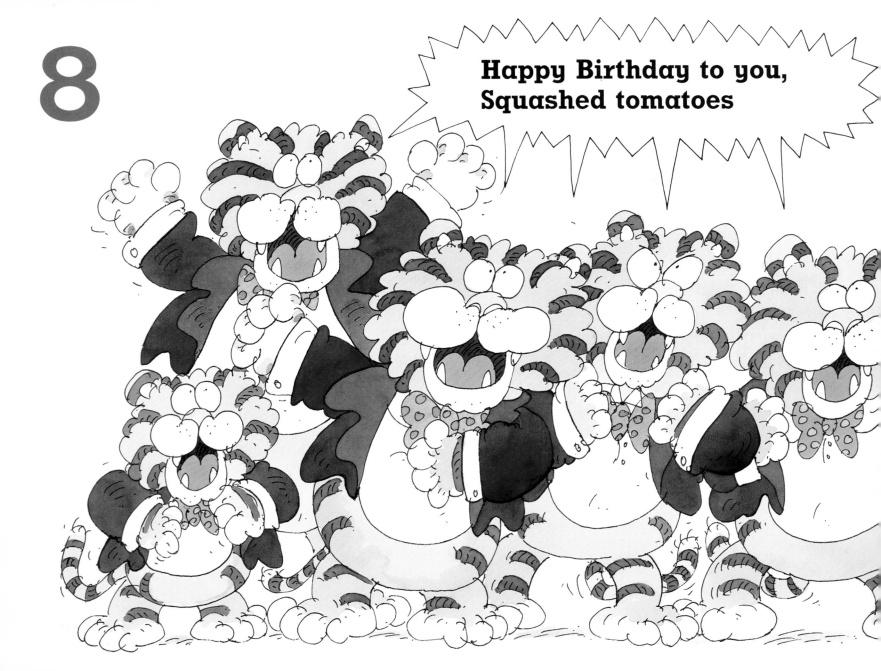

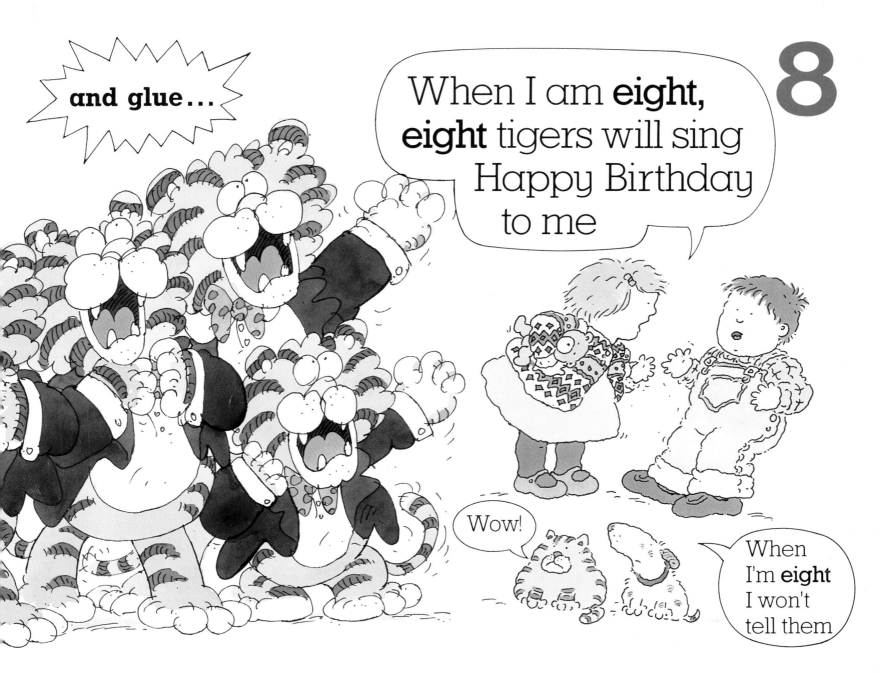

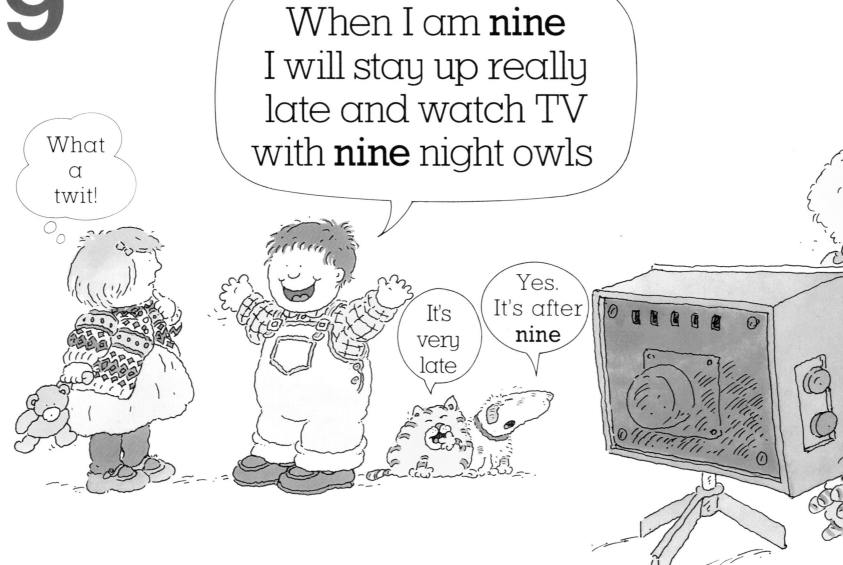

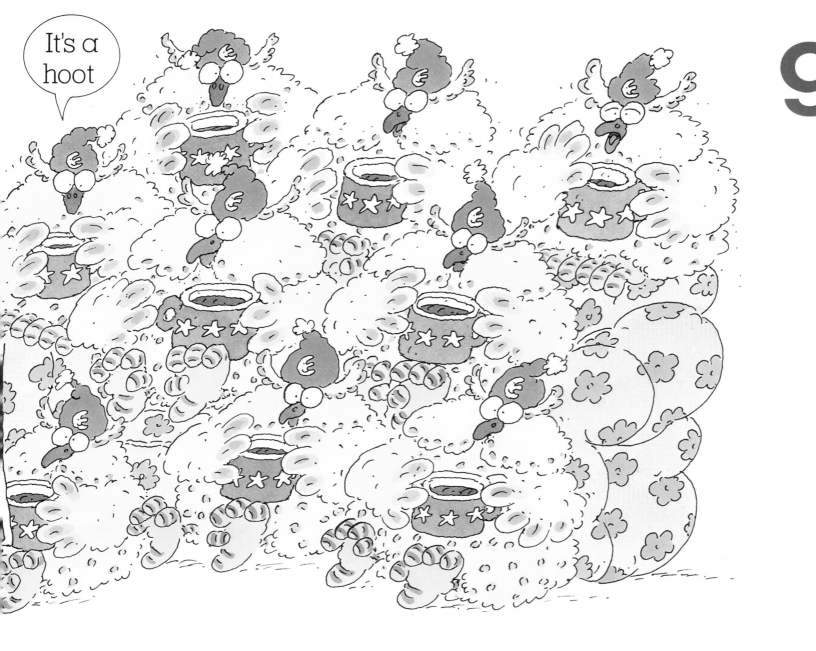

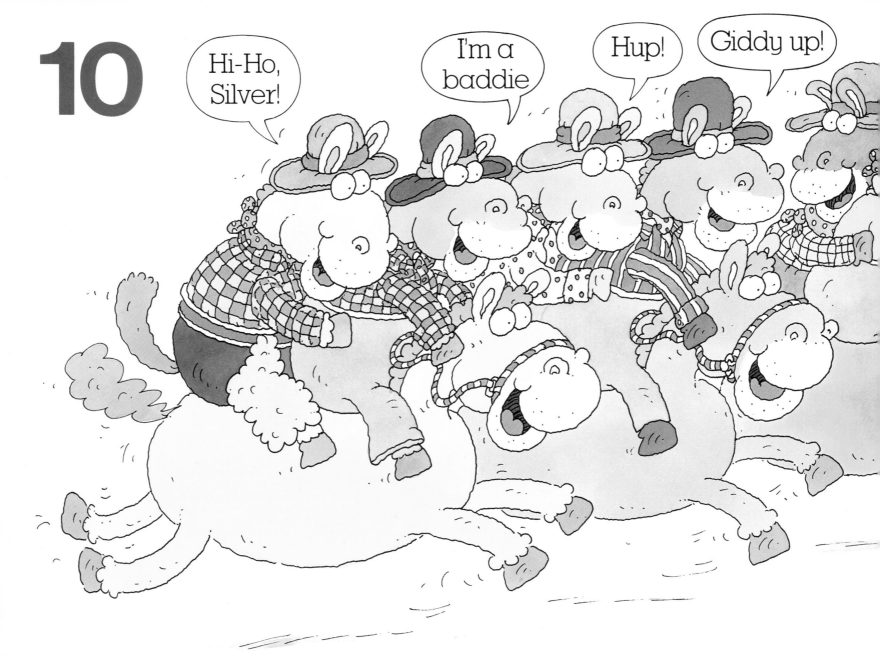

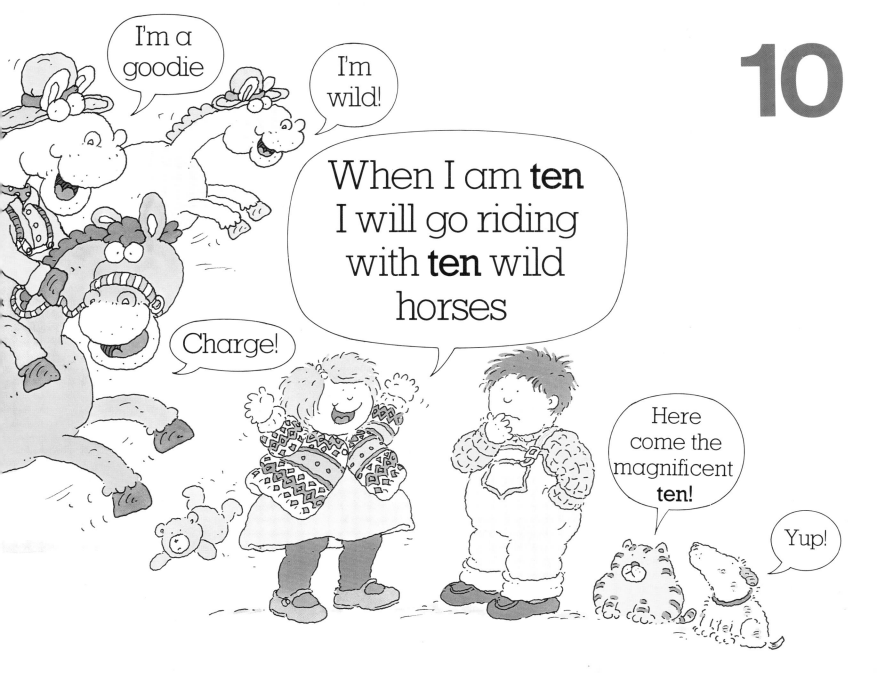

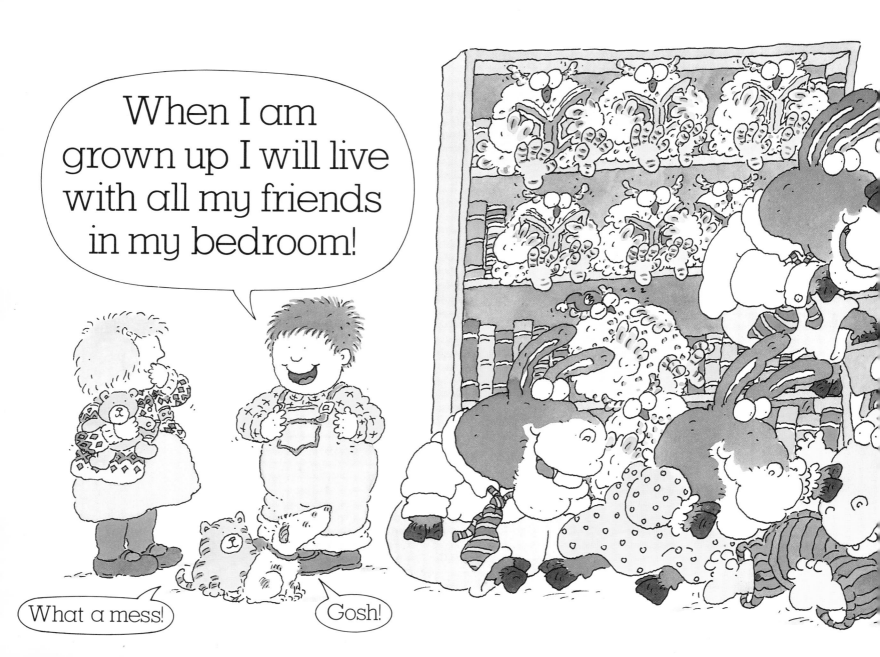

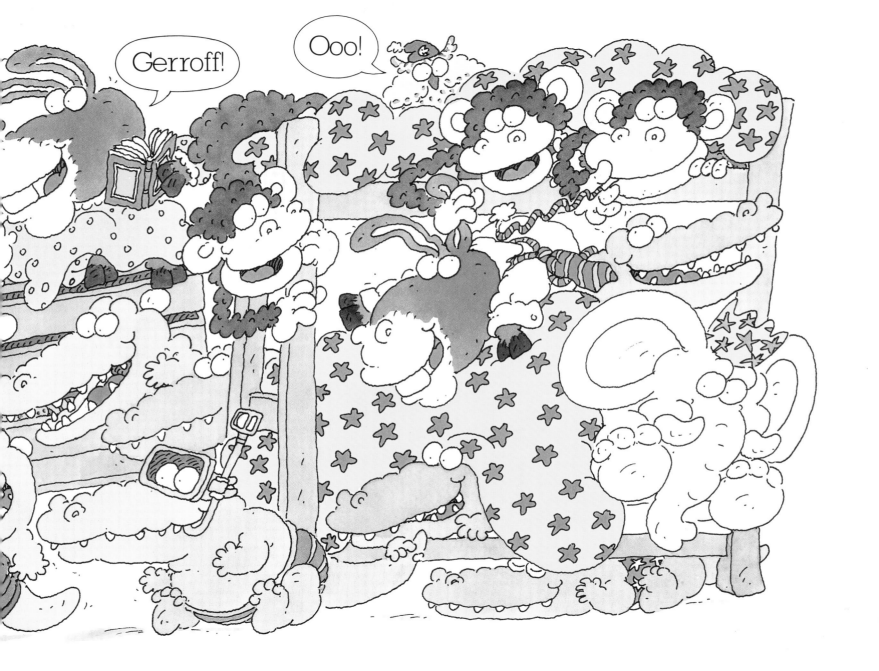

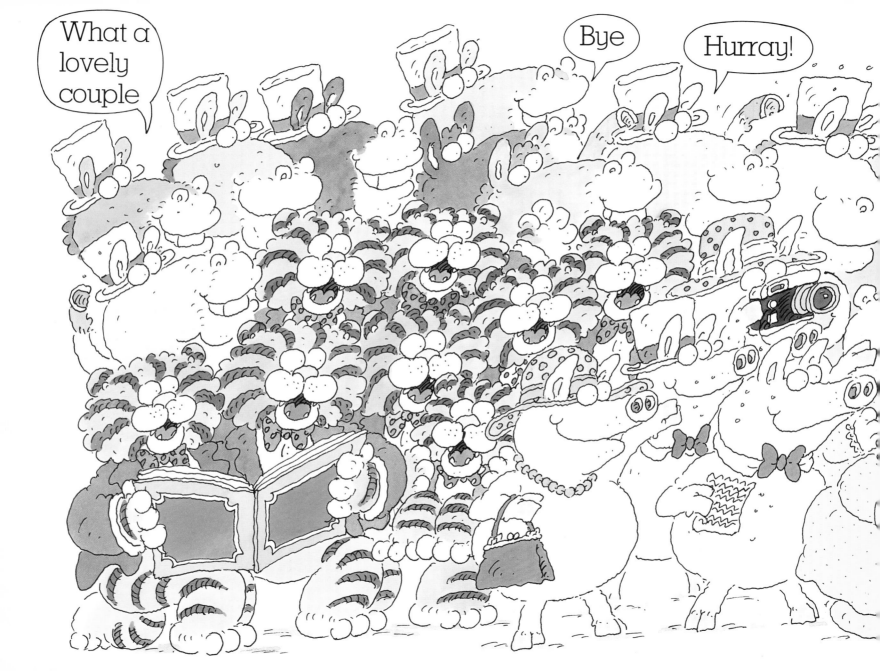

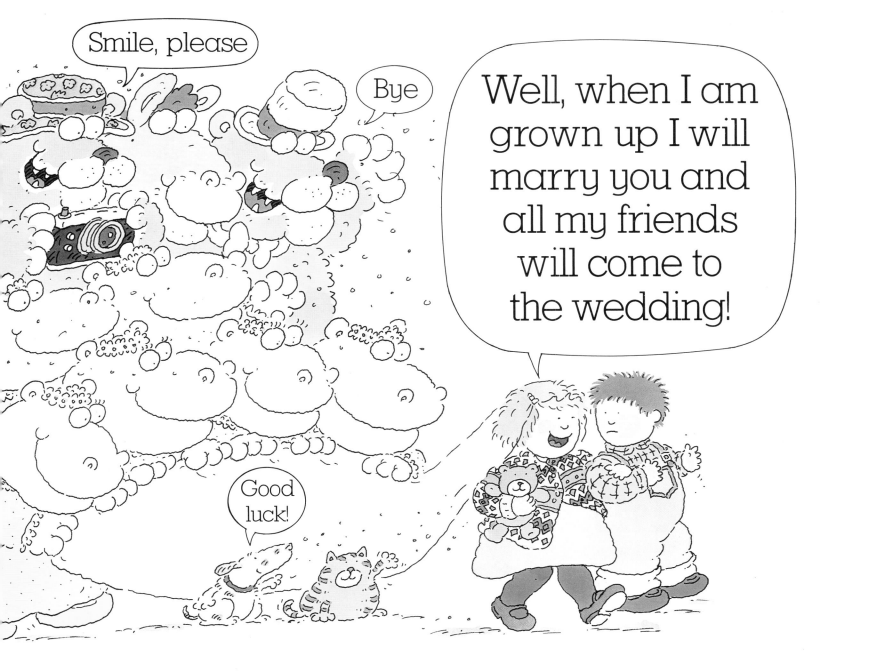

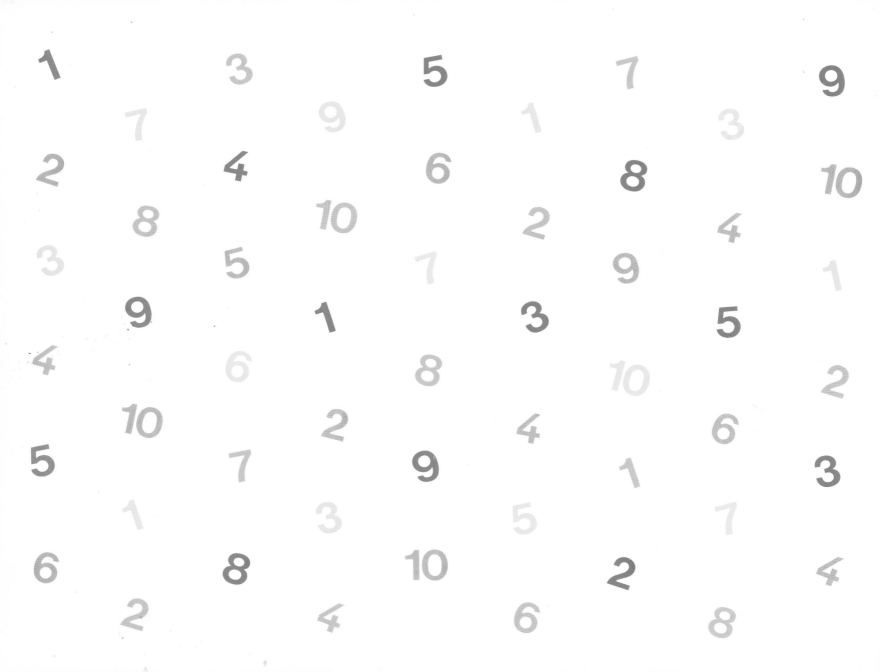